For my good friend Paeony Lewis
D B

For Heidi, Chloe, and Ben,
for their love, support, and cups of tea
D H

LITTLE TIGER PRESS LTD,
an imprint of the Little Tiger Group
1 The Coda Centre, 189 Munster Road, London SW6 6AW
www.littletiger.co.uk

First published in Great Britain 2003
This edition published 2017

ISBN 978-1-84869-757-7

A CIP catalogue record for this book is available from the British Library

Printed in China • LTP/1400/1874/0417

1 3 5 7 9 10 8 6 4 2

What Are You Doing in My Bed?

David Bedford   Daniel Howarth

LITTLE TIGER

LONDON

Kip the Kitten had nowhere to sleep
on a dark and cold winter's night.
So he crept through a door . . .

. . . and curled up warm and
snug in somebody's bed.

Then out of the dark
Kip heard . . .

. . . whispers and hisses,
and soft feet padding
through the night.

Bright green eyes peered
in through the window,
and suddenly . . .

. . . one, two, three, four, five, six cats
came banging through the cat door!
They tumbled and skidded and rolled
across the floor, where they found . . .

. . . Kip!

"What are YOU doing in OUR bed?"
shouted the six angry cats.

"Your bed?" said Kip.
"But this bed's too small for
you. You'd never all fit!"

"Never fit?" said the cats.
"Just you watch!"

One, two, three cats curled up
neatly, head to tail . . .

then four, five, six cats
piled on top.

"See? There's no room
   for you," they said.
"You'd never fit."

"Never fit?"
   said Kip.
"Just you
   watch!"

Tottering and teetering,
Kip carefully climbed on top.
"I'll sleep here," he said.

"OK," the cats yawned.
"But don't fidget or snore."
And they fell asleep in a heap.

But suddenly, a big, deep,
growly voice said . . .

"WHAT ARE YOU DOING IN MY BED? SCRAM!"

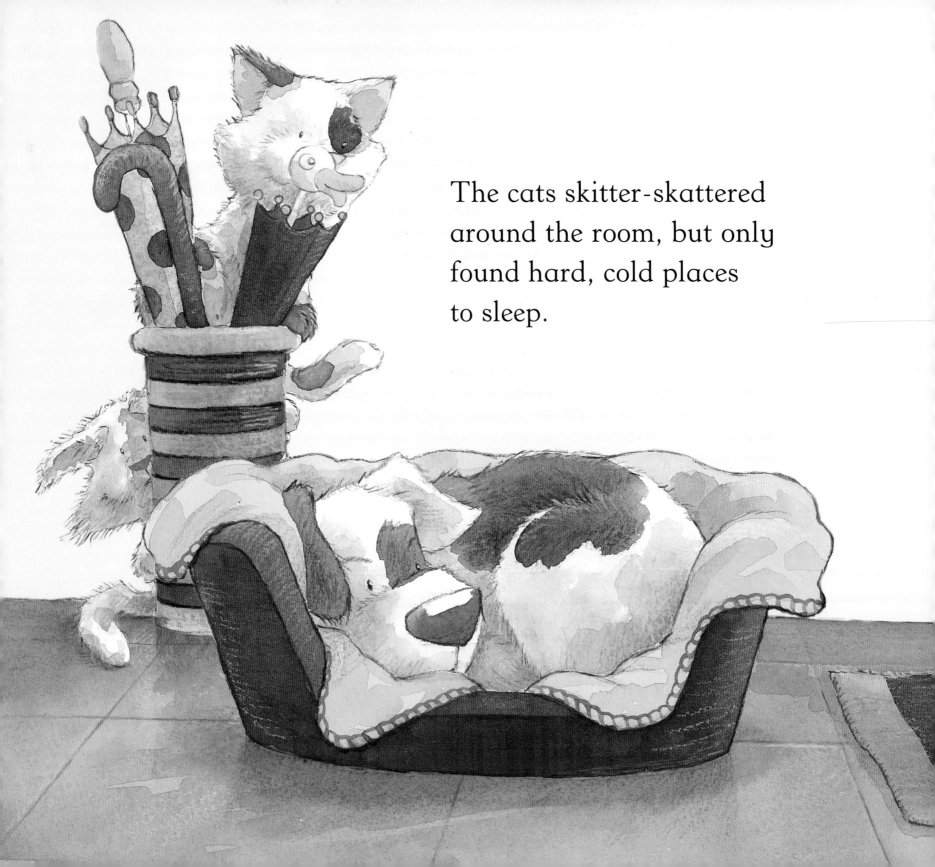

The cats skitter-skattered
around the room, but only
found hard, cold places
to sleep.

Harry the Dog was comfy in his bed,
and he soon began to snore.

But then an icy wind whistled in through
the cat door, and Harry awoke
and shivered.

Kip whispered, "Follow me . . . ,"
and he quickly led six cold cats
across the floor . . .

. . . to the cosy bed.
"We'll keep you warm,"
said Kip.

"You'll never all fit," chattered Harry.
"Never fit?" said Kip. "Just you watch!"

Kip and Harry snored right through the night under their warm blanket of cats.

And they all fitted purr-fectly!